Maddalena

Or

The Fate of the Florentines

By

Horace Walpole

British Library Cataloguing-in-Publication Data
A catalogue record for this book is available from
the British Library

Contents

HORACE WALPOLE

Horatio Walpole was born in Westminster, London in 1717. He was educated at Eton College and then King's College, Cambridge, but left for his Grand Tour of Europe (at that time an educational rite of passage for upper-class European young men) before graduating. In 1741, he became an MP for Callington in Cornwall, but he was a lazy participant in the House of Commons, preferring to devote his time to developing his forty-acre Twickenham estate, 'Strawberry Hill'. It was here that Walpole set up his own printing press, which he used to publish his tireless output of non-fictional works. In literary terms, Walpole is best-remembered for producing *The Castle of Ontario* (1764), widely regarded as the earliest example of – and manifesto for – the modern Gothic romance. Walpole succeeded to the title of Fourth Earl of Oxford in 1791, but died six years later, aged 79.

Maddalena

THERE has always been to my mind a something hallowed and mysterious – a strange shadowy hue which seems not of this world, cast over the period of the history of Europe, generally designated 'the dark ages'. The minds of the nations seemed then to have sunk beneath the terrible and undermining convulsions which they had undergone (ere the barbarian banners were triumphantly unfurled, and waved over the conquests of the Hun, the Vandal, and the Goth,) into a long, dark, dismal night of heavy and restless slumber. Their greatest efforts, inconsiderable though always daring, resembled the misdirected starts of a troubled rest. Their intelligence seems to have been as a dream to themselves, and is ever so now to us. Yet then there was the soul of bold enterprise and watchful prowess; the mailed knight and lady fair – the castle, the warden, and the armed retainers – the sternest encounters relieved by the brightness of soft eyes, and the stoniest hearts refined and purified beneath the tender influence of women's love. Then too there was the name of Petrarch and his Laura, the wild and flashing light of Ariosto's muse, and the shadowy, unearthly inspiration of the patriot poet Dante. All, and much more than all this, is circled in our eyes within a halo which shades to softer loveliness, while it does not obscure those days of old romance; elating the mind to a fond enthusiasm for its brighter, while it steeps it into a

3

willing forgetfulness of its darker and more repugnant shapes.

I remember hearing, some years ago, in the neighbourhood of Pisa, a legend of those dark yet fondly recollected times. I tell it, because it is of them, and this must be its only merit.

Everyone knows, or at least ought to know the wretched condition to which the city of Pisa was reduced about the end of the fifteenth century. Then it was that this little state almost fell a victim to the ambition, or causeless vengeance, of the Florentines; and but for a spark of high independence, her only and best inheritance of the great republic, which still lingered among the petty communities of Italy, together with a fixed and rooted hatred towards the invaders of her liberty, she would have been swept from her existence as a nation and a people.

Just on the eve of the breaking out of that concealed and bitter enmity which had long rankled in the bosoms of the two states, Florentines were to be seen in the streets of Pisa, and some of France upon the liberties of Naples had roused their animosity to its full and reckless strength, their inhabitants lived in a sort of society together, restrained and suspicious it is true, yet not without the traces of apparent friendship at least. Many Florentines were to be seen in the streets of Pisa, and some Pisans in the streets of Florence. Still the collisions, when they happened to come into collision, were far from friendly. Each scowled on the other, as if he would have given way at once to open enmity; but both were equally afraid to begin the attack. The heart's wish of the one was to have spit in the face of the other, and cry 'villain'; but somehow or other there existed for several years a sort of courtesy and restraint on both sides, which prevented this generally taking place, though sometimes it did occur.

As always happens in cases of this kind, the fair sex were sure to catch up and perpetuate the spirit of their lords. Withered matrons and spinster ladies had their national 'likes and dislikes', and along with these their feuds and bitter hostilities. In spite of all this, however, there were often little love affairs between the youth of the two cities, genial and fond, though at times burning into madness, the same as love has always appeared and now appears under the sun of Italy:

Where fiercest passion riots unconfined,
And in its madness fires the softest mind.

About this time there lived in Pisa a rich Florentine mer-
chant, by name Jacopo. He had retired many years from trade,
living quietly and contentedly on his gains. Pisa had become his
place of residence, not so much from choice as from the strong
associations with which it was connected in his mind – remin-
iscences of his early love, which his business-life and business-
habits had all been unable to efface. Pisa had been the birthplace
of his wife, and the first scene of the first and fondest affection
he had ever known. There too the curtain had dropped, and left
him widowed in heart and life. It was to him therefore as the en-
chanter's palace of light and darkness, which he would gladly
have avoided, but which he found it impossible to tear himself
from. He clung to it, as the spirit of an injured maid is said, in
the old legends, to linger round the scene of her ruin. Those
who have had the links of earliest and consequently most
powerful love snapt asunder ere well united, alone know the
feelings which still through life attach themselves to the scene
of its first raptures, even though its original brightness may
afterwards have been dimmed by becoming the scene of its
bitterest desolation.

His wife died little more than a year after they had been
united, leaving Jacopo a daughter. On this solitary pledge of his
wedded love, all his attention had been lavished, and no expense
spared; so that when Maddalena attained the age of woman-
hood there was scarcely a more accomplished, and not a more
beautiful and gentle maiden to be found in the whole of Pisa.
She was the image of her mother in figure, mind, and temper;
and this had bound, if possible, more closely the ties of paternal
affection. Jacopo, in the warmth of his love had never allowed her
to leave his sight, or at least to be far from him. She was seldom
to be met with in the public places, to which, in those days, the
youth of her age so generally resorted. The lists, the dance, and
the marriage feast were seldom graced by her presence; and
even when she did make her appearance there, it was more as a

spectator than a partaker in their gaieties; for Jacopo, though he lived in that dissolute age, knew and dreaded the danger to which youth and beauty are exposed to in their communion with the world.

Under the protection and guidance of this fatherly solicitude, Maddalena had arrived at the age of seventeen, and her heart was still her own. Many of the richest nobles of Pisa had made proposals for her hand, which Jacopo had deemed it prudent to refuse. Nay, scarce was there a finger in all Pisa that could touch the lute, which was not, some night, or other of the year, sweeping its chords beneath her latticed window. She used to smile as she heard the serenades to her own beauty, at times admiring the musicians skill, and sometimes blushing as she heard herself, in the same stanza compared to the rose, the lily, and the morning star.

One night in December – it was a cold and silent night, and the moon was up, which steeped, as it were, the pure white marble of Pisa in her own still purer and whiter light – Maddalena sat alone in her panelled chamber, in anxious expectation of the return of her father, who had been absent for some hours. The moonlight, streaming through the casement at which she sat, fell full and bright on the picture of an old crusader, giving a shadowy and unusual look to the countenance. This, together with the wild imagery of one of the Provençal ballads she had been reading, deeply embued her mind with a melancholy and tender feeling. She threw down the ballad – she gazed on the bold and rugged outlines of the warrior's face – she attempted again to read – she desisted – and her eyes were riveted on the dark contour of the warrior's countenance, made more striking by the moonlight which rested upon it. Her mind could not settle. The hour and the scene altogether had wrought her up into that feverish feeling of romance which all young hearts have known, and they the most who have held least intercourse with the world.

While she continued in this state, half in pleasure, half in pain, the tones of a lute, in a slow and solemn Italian air, softly arose from below the casement at which she sat. At first the musician's fingers seemed scarcely to touch the chords. A single note was only now and then heard, like the distant murmur of a stream in the desert; then it gradually rose, and rose, and swelled into deeper softness, till the music at length burst into all the voluptuousness of perfect melody. Love could not have fixed upon a better hour to insinuate himself into the most impenetrable heart. A maid alone and in moonlight, with her senses floating on the lovely sounds of music, and her heart steeped in romantic feeling, rather woos than shuns his approaches; and we need scarcely inform our readers of either sex that so it was with Maddalena. – While the stranger sung in a clear and manly voice the words of a plaintive canzonetta, she drew back the casement, and half afraid, yet anxious to catch a glimpse of the musician, she leant herself timidly over it. The minstrel's eyes were fixed intently on the spot where she was; and when he saw her gently open the lattice, the notes of his lute seemed to swell into greater rapture, continuing on the air even after the musician had ceased. Maddalena could perceive, standing in a shadow of the moonlight, occasioned by a projecting part of the building, a young cavalier, wrapt in a loose cloak, and underneath it and across his breast one of those old fashioned lutes which we may see every day represented in the prints of the wandering Troubadours. The youth sighed, looked fondly, knelt, and talked of love. She spoke not, but she listened.

We write not for the stupid elf, squire, or dame, who has yet to be told that love needs but a beginning; or who cannot guess, till they have it staring them out of countenance in black and white, that Borgiano (for so the youth was called) and Maddalena were lovers before a week had past. It is time, however, to inform our readers that the youth was of Florentine extraction; that he had come to Pisa to avail himself of her schools, which had even then obtained great celebrity throughout Europe; and that he was in the middle of his studies when the incident which we have related took place.

Love, more perhaps in Italy than in any other country, has

always had free liberty to run its own course. Plant it but in two bosoms, and they are sure, in spite of the keenest vigilance, to have their meetings, their sighs, and their oaths. Jacopo knew no more of what was going on between his daughter and Borgiano than the nightingale which sat and sang above the bower, the scene of their earliest and only interview. Women, if the truth must be told, were then the same as they are now; daughters, in love matters, cheated their grey-haired fathers, and wives not infrequently their fatherly husbands.

Jacopo had been invited one evening to the house of the nobles, where several of the principal men of Pisa were assembled. Meali Lanfranchi, one of these, had paid court to the old gentleman, and completely cheated him out of his affection. A proposal was made by him for the hand of Maddalena, which was readily enough agreed to by Jacopo, who saw no reason, nor did he rack his brain for any, why he should not unite himself in the person of his daughter with the first of the Pisan nobility. Meali was a branch of the Lanfranchi family, one of the oldest and most powerful in the state. He had lived but little in his native place, and having newly returned to it after a long absence, he was, of course, the theme of much and general observation. His faults were either altogether unknown, or glossed over in the novelty of his return; and whether it was that Jacopo was dazzled with his rank, or captivated by his address, it was agreed before they parted that an interview should take place on the following day. Lanfranchi, satisfied with the progress he had made, went exulting to his palace, and Jacopo, musing and chuckling all the way over the elevation which he fondly anticipated for his daughter. He found her in a thoughtful mood, and waiting his return.

Borgiano had that evening made a more open avowal of his love than he had hitherto done. He had sworn his plighted faith, and had entreated a return from her; but however pleasing the request might be, it had distressed Maddalena. It was true she loved him, yet she had scarcely ever dared to own it to herself. With the strange caprice of every maiden who loves for the first time, she had dwelt with fond delight on her affection, and everything connected with it, when alone, and when it was seen only in the lights and shadows which fancy chose to bestow. Yet when her lover made the avowal, which she could not but expect, she was strangely disconcerted, and even depressed in spirits. In this state Jacopo found her on his arrival at home.

'Maddalena,' he said, patting her at the same time under the chin, 'what would you say, Maddalena, if you were now to become a wife?'

'A wife, father?'

'Aye, a wife, Maddalena; and a wife to the first noble in Pisa. What think you of that, my girl?'

'I think, father; I only think I would rather be your child than wife to the first noble in all the world.'

'Well, well, Maddalena, your affection is not unreturned, and I like you not the worse for this coyness; 'tis your sex's best failing. But we shall talk more of it tomorrow, when your lover comes. And then, my girl, when he is here, there will be soft words and stolen glances. You will be gay as a lark in a May morning, and your lover – but good night, good night,' he said, suddenly stopping when he saw that his daughter took little heed of the rhapsody he was pouring upon her ears; and imprinting a paternal kiss upon her cheek, which had flushed into a burning crimson when she heard him talk of the morrow and a lover, he left her to herself.

Next morning Lanfranchi, punctual to a moment, was at the house of his new friend Jacopo, who of course received him with the kindest welcome. – Maddalena stood with her arm leant upon the lattice, her eye turned to the broad expanse of field and vineyard, gradually lessening perspectively till they joined in with the blue towering Appenines in the distance: and, strange for a female in the immediate presence of an avowed lover to whom she had no heart to give, she looked all unconcern. But it was only the appearance of a command, and not a real mastery which she possessed over her feelings. And Lanfranchi, though a man of the world, and little accustomed to lay any restraint upon his inclinations, felt confused under the composed look and commanding beauty of Maddalena. She ventured to cast but one glance on her professed suitor. He was a man apparently about thirty years of age, with a keen grey eye, whose expression, though subdued at present, seemed rather of command than of entreaty, and suited well with the dark and overshadowing mass of his eyebrows. A green silk doublet, bespangled with gold, hung down from his shoulder, and in his hand he bore a round cap of the same colour, which was ornamented with an eagle's feather.

When Jacopo, in order to give him an opportunity of declaring himself, had left the apartment, Lanfranchi changed immediately his former awkwardness and want of confidence for the manner and freedom of a man who had only to speak in order to be obeyed. Gazing on Maddalena with the licentious look of a professed libertine, he seized her by the hand, and poured forth a torrent of vows and protestations. The maid gave a sort of involuntary shudder, and started back, but Lanfranchi still pressing his suit, attempted to put his arm around her waist.

'Is this the manner, Sir, you repay my father's kindness, by insult to his daughter?' she said and she accompanied these words with a look of offended dignity, which for a moment confused Lanfranchi, and ere he could recover from his surprise, she left the apartment.

Jacopo, as he entered the room, smiling, smirking, and looking sufficiently wise, found Lanfranchi standing as if a spell had hardened every limb of him to stone. But whatever the old man's thoughts were, he determined to remain silent on the subject till the other should inform him of what had passed. Lanfranchi, however, bade him adieu, without adverting even to the object of his visit, but not without many invitations from Jacopo to return on the morrow. The morrow came, and so did Lanfranchi; but Maddalena remained inflexible in never leaving her apartment as long as his visits lasted. She was convinced that her father would never force her into a marriage so much against her inclination. All this time (what will not love effect?) Borgiano and the maiden had their stolen interviews, and surely not the less delightful that they were stolen. Often, when all were at rest, and the moon threw her faint light across their path, they wandered in the garden, which sloped beautifully down to the banks of the river. There daybreak often found them, and that hour – the loveliest hour of all – when the sun rises from behind the Appenines, like a new-born spirit starting from the mountain tops, and his freshened beams rest on the glittering rocks of Carrara and the white marble buildings of Pisa, or float on the green waves of the far-rolling Tuscan sea – that hour was the least beloved by them, for it told of parting.

Matters were in this situation when the report of the invasion of Charles the Eighth of France, who had already entered the Italian frontier, spread consternation far and wide throughout the whole land. Some beheld in this wild and ambitious scheme, the foreboding clouds of that ruin and desolation which, a month or two afterwards, it spread over the fairest cities in Italy. Others, who with reason or from imagination looked upon their wretchedness as already beyond the possibility of being increased, turned to the Gallic invader as to a saving angel, and flocked to do him homage.

The gradual and ambitious encroachments made upon the territories of Pisa by the Florentines, had, previously to Charles's invasion, kindled into a flame those sparks of enmity which had so long lain smothered in the bosoms of the two states. Pisa had now taken the alarm, but as yet ventured upon no act of open hostility. She lay like a tigress in her den, determined to avoid any offensive measures on her part, but resolved to offer the firmest resistance to any assault upon her liberty. She knew that her ill-disciplined and worse organized army formed but a feeble barrier against the regular condottiere of Florence. This consciousness of her own weakness, more, perhaps, than any other consideration, served to continue, so long, her sullen and unwilling forebearance.

To her inhabitants in such a state of mind, Providence seemed to have interposed in directing Charles's march across the Alps. Scarcely, therefore, had he quitted Lucca on his way to this city, when its inhabitants gathered around him, pouring forth the most tumultuous expressions of their joy, and hailing him as the saviour of their country. The wavering and deceitful policy of this monarch, whose good deeds seldom went farther than the promise, was not wanting on the present occasion. He met the ardent solicitations of the Pisans, and gave them the assurance of his protection. This favourable reply raised them from the lowest despondency into the wildest exultation. Regarding it as their emancipation from slavery, they broke forth into the utmost excesses; every badge which distinguished the Florentines throughout the city was demolished: and it might well be said, that the matin bell of liberty to the one state pealed a death note on the ear of the other.

Jacopo was within the sphere of this persecution, but on account of his age, and the influence he possessed with many of the nobles, he was allowed two days to deliberate whether he should leave the city unmolested, or brave the fury of the populace, by remaining within its walls. Lanfranchi had all along continued his suit to Maddalena, with as little success as he had at first commenced it; though his addresses had assumed a more determined tone, and he demanded her union with him, more as if he were condescending on his part than she granting a favour on hers.

On the night after Charles had made his entrance into Pisa, Lanfranchi came to the house of Jacopo. He was dressed out as a reveller, and indeed from his eye and gait, it was evident he had lately risen from a company of Bacchanals. The old man, attended by his daughter, sat in an apartment the farthest from the street, (for not a Florentine dared to be seen), whose dark hangings and sombre tapestry gave a melancholy hue to the faces of its inmates, and contrasted strangely with the gay colours of Lanfranchi's dress. As the old man rose to receive him, his guest seemed to cast upon them both the eye of a serpent, which already has its prey within its power; – pityless, remorseless, determined, – his look was like that of one, whose word carried life or death. Jacopo seemed almost to tremble under his scowl, and the heart of Maddalena almost leapt from its seat as her eye met his.

'Cheer up, good father,' said Lanfranchi in a merry tone –

Maddalena

'Nay, look not so dull, man, ne'er a dog in all Pisa dares to bite when I say hold; and the boldest hand in the city shall not touch a single hair of that white head of thine if I say no.'

The old man remained silent.

'Rouse thee, man, or I shall think thee coward if thou quakest so. As father of my bride, I pledge my word you shall be safe were you ten Florentines, aye, by the holy virgin, were you ten thousand Florentines.'

At this last sentence, the tears burst forth from Maddalena's eyes.

'What! weeping and groans on a bridal eve? Throw them away, my pretty ladybird, we shall have no clouds over our honeymoon:' continued Lanfranchi in the same tone – and advancing to where Maddalena was sitting, he attempted to put his arm round her neck but she repelled him – 'Desist, sir; for though you were hateful to me in your prosperity you are doubly so in our distress.'

Lanfranchi burst into a scornful laugh – 'How pretty the fair thing looks in a passion; by my faith she might enact tragedy.'

Jacopo's blood was fired within him, at this last insult.

'Villain!' cried the old man, – 'dost thou think to trample upon us in our misery; and triumph over us in our misfortunes? She shall never be yours.'

'Villain – ha – villain; I think that was the word you used. Why you miserable dotard – villain, forsooth – a gentleman can't make love to your daughter, and tell her how beautiful she is, but you must call him – villain! Hark you, old man, you have been drinking freely, and I pardon you; besides, there's not a Florentine now in the city that does not hate us Pisans. I tell you plainly, your daughter shall be mine tomorrow!'

'Never! never!' exclaimed Maddalena.

'Hush! peace! my pretty prattler. By tomorrow's night she shall be mine, old man, or death may chance to you, and worse perhaps to her.'

'Holy virgin!' said Maddalena, kneeling before a small image of the Madonna, 'shield his grey hairs – save, oh save my father; let not him die for the misfortune of his daughter.'

13

A pretty enough orison, and prettily told,' said Lanfranchi, scornfully; 'but even that will scarcely save you.'

Maddalena still knelt; her hands were clasped over her face, down which her tears fell heavy and fast.

Lanfranchi looked upon her more with the eye of wild licentious appetite than of love; more of keen-searching mockery than of pity.

'Pray on,' he said, 'aye, pray loud, and well too; it may be the last prayer your father can partake in.'

'Have you no pity?' exclaimed Maddalena, seizing at the same time, with both hands, the corner of his doublet; 'Spare him – stain not your hands with his blood. – I am your victim, slay but me, heaven will pardon you the murder.'

'That may be all in good time, thou prattler,' Lanfranchi replied, in a deep calm tone of voice; and tearing his doublet from her hands, he left the house.

When he was gone, the father and the daughter remained silent. The old man's thoughts of himself and his own safety were drowned in one resistless and prevailing feeling of horror for the wretch who had just left them. He thought but of the villain that interview had disclosed; to whom, but a day before, he would have given his daughter in preference to any other. Maddalena's emotions were not so easily concentrated in one point. The man whom she had always before regarded with indifference; as one whom, as she could not love, she could easily cast off; now appeared to her in all the colours of a demon, crying aloud for her father's blood and her destruction. But wretched and pitiable as was her present condition, she attempted to comfort her father, who had sunk upon his knees in a state of terrible bewilderment. The old man rose as she addressed him; he had no heart to speak. His dim eye, on which a tear swam, like a cloud of vapour hanging over a dying light, the last of a deserted hall, told more than his tongue could utter. 'Good night, Maddalena, good night, and heaven be your protector;' said Jacopo as he embraced his daughter. 'God have mercy,' answered Maddalena, as he left the apartment.

When the maiden was left alone, and her mind was distracted

between the thoughts which tempested within her breast; then, indeed, she felt the anguish of a horror-haunted spirit. – When she thought of her approaching doom, and her own miserable situation, she fancied the cup of her grief was full. But when she recurred to Borgiano, and thought of their love and their misfortunes, her spirit died within her. Then she reverted to the horrors threatened to her by Lanfranchi, and an icy coldness crept around her heart, like one who stands on the outermost verge of a tottering precipice, chained to the spot without the power of escaping. And was there really no way of saving themselves? she thought, and at last resolved to go to the house of a Pisan lady, at a short distance, and consult with her on the likeliest means of escape.

She seated herself at the latticed window; her eyes rested, but all unconscious of its beauties, on the splendid night scene which lay stretched before her. The moon shone over the vine rows, the palaces, and hanging tower of Pisa, resting on the calm, clear wave which almost slumbered on the shore close by; for the sea had not then, as it has now, like a capricious mistress, abandoned this delightful city; while the nightingale, seated on top branch of an olive tree, seemed to 'tune its sad heart to music.' But these had no pleasure for Maddalena's mind. Her mind rolled unobserving over the beauties of the one, and her ear was not attuned to the melody of the other. She had remained in this situation but a short time, when the figure of a man appeared below the window at which she sat. It was Borgiano. He beckoned her to speak; but ere she could undo the casement, he had fled, and immediately a crowd of Pisans ran shouting up the same path he had taken. When the confusion was past, and all was again silent, Maddalena, wrapping herself in one of those long folding mantles, so common a part of the ladies' dress in the fifteenth and sixteenth centuries, glided with light and anxious steps along the gallery leading from her apartment into the street. Even in that hour of darkness, (for it was already far past midnight), the ways were crowded with groups of Pisans, and resounded with the burst of their boisterous revelry. With trembling step and fearful heart, she hurried past the assemblages of riotous nobility and drunken rabble, which in every corner stopped her passage; and, luckily no one attempted to interrupt her, till she arrived in safety at the top of the avenue, from which she had a view of Lanfranchi's palace. She raised the hood and veil which hid her face, retiring at the same time beneath a portico at one corner of the street. While she stood here, looking down upon the palace below, which shone with a thousand coloured lights, and from which she heard the sounds of Wassail, and the dull loud notes of music, an individual in a loose riding cloak, with a mask over his face, approached her. Maddalena drew forward her veil, but the stranger had already recognized her. 'You are a Florentine, and daughter of the rich Jacopo;' he said, in a low voice.

'May I ask,' replied Maddalena, 'who the stranger is that takes an interest in my fate?' – as she spoke, she again walked on.

'Stay!' said the other, seizing her by the arm 'are you mad thus to run heedless to your own destruction? Fly! another hour in this city! the death hounds are abroad; and woe to every Florentine that shall then be found in Pisa. These are not the words of a man who has any interest in you or in anyone more than common humanity.' The maid knew not what to say, or what course to follow. She had no reason to distrust the stranger; yet at that moment she was little inclined to place confidence in anyone. While she remained in this uncertainty, several individuals, clad in bright armour, issued from the palace, and entered the avenue, at the top of which Maddalena and the stranger stood.

'Haste with me, maiden,' he said anxiously, 'or all is lost.'

She remained mute and motionless; she had not the power to move. This last adventure had completely worn out her already exhausted spirits. In the meantime the stranger raised her up in his arms, and hastened with her down a narrow passage, leading from that part of the city to its suburbs. They had scarcely entered in, when the voices of those they had already seen, were heard distinctly as they passed along the avenue.

'Now for the old Florentine, Jacopo!' said one.

'Take him,' said another, 'flesh, blood, bones, and all: give me his coffers, my staunch hearts, and you may hack, and hew, and divide his anatomy amongst you.'

'Coffers!' interrupted a third, 'curse the old dotard and his gold; give me but –'

'What?' said a gruff voice.

'The sweet little jewel that decks his casket.'

'A mere lapidary; shut his mouth!' said, or rather bellowed the same rough voice, and a hoarse laugh ran through the whole party.

'Aye, laugh on,' said the other, 'but this bright jewel shall be mine; this lady rose-bud; this daughter of the Florentine.'

'Bah;' said he of the gruff voice, 'the girl shall be mine; I've sworn it on my sword: and whoso makes me break my oath, must break its blade too.'

The sound of their voices gradually dying away as they passed on, their conversation was no longer audible. The stranger, in the meantime, hurried on with Maddalena, sometimes supporting her in his arms, at other times assisting her as she walked almost unconsciously along the path he conducted her. At length they reached an old massy ruin, the solitary remnant of a former age, where were already assembled a crowd of Florentines. Amongst them there were several females, many with their clothes loosely thrown about them, some bearing in their arms half naked children, and all of them in tears. When Maddalena and her conductor arrived, they were just upon the point of setting forth upon their journey. She was mounted on a quiet pony, along side of which the stranger rode; leading it by the reins, and at the same time assisting the maiden to retain her seat. With several other ladies, apparently of distinction, she was placed in the troop of armed horsemen; all the time unconscious of where she was, or of the part she was acting. Thus prepared, the party rode on at a sharp pace in the direction of Florence.

They chose, for greater security, a lonely and sequestered road along the banks of the river Arno. The rapid motion with which she was hurried forward, somewhat brought Maddalena to herself. 'My father! where is my father?' were the first words she uttered.

'Fear not, he is safe,' said the person who conducted her. There was no time for further conversation on either side, for as they turned up a road which led round a little bend formed by the river, they were met by a party of armed Pisans. 'Pisans!' ran in whispers round the whole of the one party. 'Arm, arm my brave hearts!' shouted the other. In a moment or two all was in an uproar — the men on either side attacked, and were attacked, while the clash of their arms was mingled with the screams of the women.

The stroke of a halbert, aimed at her conductor, slightly grazed the shoulder of Maddalena; and slight as the blow was, it was sufficient in her enfeebled state to fell her to the ground. This encounter ended as encounters generally did at that time, especially in Italy, where more blows were given than blood spilt, and more booty taken than lives lost. In the present instance, as each Pisan struck his adversary to the ground, he took from him what most pleased his fancy, and then galloped off, leaving his companions to provide for themselves. Maddalena became the prize of one of these, not, however, before her conductor, who persisted in defending her, was fell to the earth by a mortal wound. In falling, the mask dropped from his face, and revealed to Maddalena the features of a faithful domestic, who had lived in her father's family several years before. She was hurried again towards the city with even more rapidity than she had left it. When again within its walls, she was led to one of the prisons, where many Florentines had that night been shut up. As they passed along the damp gallery, a dismal groan arose from the floor of the passage which conducted to her cell. The light of a torch, which was carried by one of the attendants, discovered the body of a man apparently in the writhings of death, stretched across her path. As she passed him, the dying man took firm hold of Maddalena's foot with his hand. The others attempted to disengage his grip, but it was clenched in a death grasp. Maddalena still possessed her senses enough to be able to discover the mangled form of the expiring wretch who held her

to the spot, and to see the dark clotted blood in which he wel-
tered. At the sight she staggered where she stood, and uttering
one of those wild hysteric screams, which anyone who has once
heard a woman utter can never forget, she fell senseless to the
ground. A Pisan of the party severed the hand and arm from the
body; for a while it still clung to her foot, as the others carried
her within the cell; where, laying her on a stone bench which
ran along the wall, they left her in a death-like stupor, to live or
die.

Charles the Eighth, though fond in the extreme of all the
pomp and display of chivalry, possessed few of the milder and
more refined shades of character, which, in its early existence,
distinguished that splendid institution. A species of absurd van-
ity often drowned in him even the common feelings, which are
seldom altogether extinguished in any breast, imparting to some
parts of his character a dismal hue of tyranny and oppression,
while it stamped others with an appearance of weakness and im-
becility. In spite of all this, he was not devoid, when freed from
this his worst and greatest failing, of the seeds of a more ele-
vated mind, which, had it never felt the contagion of despotic
royalty and its power, might have ripened into better fruit than
it ever bore in him His best virtue was, perhaps, a strong commiseration for the miseries of which his ambition was the cause,
and a consequent desire of repairing them.

A feeling of this sort came over him when he was informed of
the outrages committed on the Florentines; and next morning,
forgetting the pleasures to which he was naturally so prone, he
rode through the streets of Pisa, attended by a party of armed
knights, commanding the prisoners to be immediately released.
Among the number of miserable prisons which the monarch
visited in person, was the one into which Maddalena had been
thrown the evening before. Accompanied by two knights of his
retinue, he entered the cell where she sat, or rather lay, on the
stone bench which was formed out of the body of the wall. The
lower part of her garment was soaked in blood, her face was as
pale as ashes, and her eyes being closed, it seemed as if she was
in sound untroubled sleep.

'A pretty chaffinch this,' whispered one of his attendants in the ear of the king; 'is't not a shame to see so pretty a bird in so rascally a cage?'

'By my knighthood, 'tis,' replied the monarch in an equally low tone of voice.

'Methinks these white lips,' replied the other, 'would grow redder beneath a kiss – shall I taste them out of courtesy to your majesty?'

'Out upon thee for a recreant knight! – can I not taste them, think ye, myself?'

As he spoke, the monarch leaning forward imprinted a kiss on Maddalena's cheek. She started up, and looked wildly round her – her large blue eyes were dim, but even then not without expression.

'Ha! there's blood upon thee!' the poor girl exclaimed; 'see – there, you have murdered Jacopo – go wash thyself – thou hast too gay a look!'

The monarch spoke some words of comfort to her, taking her at the same time by the hand.

'Let me see thee,' said Maddalena, in a hollow disconnected voice, and looking closely into his face. 'I'faith, a sprightly executioner to kill an old man and then his daughter. There's an old song – but I've forgot it now: I used to sing it long ago, and Borgiano liked it – no, no, I don't mean Borgiano – Jacopo liked it, but – they're all dead! all dead!

> With crimson drops his grey hairs dripp'd,
> For they murdered the good old man!
> The knights they danced, the ladies tripp'd,
> As they murdered the poor old man!
> Then sadly sing, heigh ho! sweetheart!
> They've murdered the poor old man.'

'A sad song for so lovely a songstress!' said one of the attendants to the monarch.

'Some love-go-mad girl,' said the other, 'some Florent –'

'Hush!' interrupted the king, 'this is no subject for ribald mirth.'

'Mirth!' said the broken-spirited girl, casting her body at the same time into a sort of capricious bend, and smiling; 'mirth, my love-a-lady – aye, there shall be mirth, and laughter, and smiles, when this poor heart shall have broken utterly. We shall sing, and be happy, and free from care, when all of us meet again, Jacopo, Borgiano, and I. Nay, look not so dull – your bride is not dead. Hark! there she sings, light o' heart – she is beckoning you. – Go!'

Less, probably, than those of any other man of his day, had Charles's feelings been exposed to the appeals of human misery. The pitiable condition of this wretched girl roused his deepest commiseration; and 'albeit unused to the melting mood,' he turned away from the melancholy spectacle, and fairly wept.

'Nay, weep not for me,' she said in a more connected tone than she had hitherto used; 'all, all are gone who loved me, or whom I loved – and I must weep when I would often sing.'

She spoke in such a note of settled sorrow, and such a look of placid composure still seemed to float over her destitution, that the monarch could not command his feelings enough to speak. While he stood thus mute and pitying, his eyes intently fixed on the still beautiful face and form of the unfortunate maniac, Jacopo rushed into the apartment. He ran to his daughter, but she started wildly back from his embrace.

'Do you not know your father?' said the old man; 'I am your father – speak to me Maddalena!' – 'You! you cannot be my father,' exclaimed the girl, 'his hair was as white as snow, and yours is red with blood! look how the blood drips from it – my old father's blood and Borgiano's.'

'My child! my child!' the old man cried in an agony of heart.

'This is indeed too much for him to bear!' said the monarch, supporting at the same time Jacopo, whose inward feeling had completely overpowered his strength. Maddalena came up to him as he lay fainting in the arms of the king.

'Sad heart, he has lost his father too; perhaps they have murdered his lady-love, as they did my Borgiano. We shall weep together over our misfortunes; aye, and sing to ease our hearts.'

By the order of the monarch, the still insensible Jacopo was borne out of the apartment. From this state of lethargy he never totally recovered, lingering on in the same miserable condition for several days till at length he expired. Once only, immediately before his death, when his soul, as it were, found a resting place between light and darkness, he recovered for a moment to a sense of his afflictions. In this brief period, he had called frequently on the name of his daughter, and accused Lanfranchi as the murderer of himself and her.

Charles himself assisted in conveying Maddalena from her dungeon; and, save that her cheek was pale, and her eye was at one time moveless, and at another rolled wildly, she was still as beautiful as ever. A weeping fit, which had succeeded in the capriciousness of her mind's disorder, the wilder ebullitions of the moment before, had tamed her look into that state of meaningless quiescence, the most distressful condition in which anyone can witness a fellow creature, especially as it was in the present instance, in the case of a beautiful young woman.

As they were slowly conducting her along, they were met at the prison-door by Borgiano, who having been freed along with the other Florentines, took the earliest opportunity of inquiring after the fate of Maddalena.

We shall not attempt to describe their meeting. Even he was unrecognized. All may imagine, though none can adequately describe the utter loneliness of heart, the agony and the despair which fell upon Borgiano, as he saw his fondest hopes blighted; and when he beheld the face upon which in happier hours he had delighted to gaze, now causelessly brightening into a smile, and now clouded with a tear, giving him the maddening assurance that her mind was gone for ever.

In the retirement to which she was conducted, her frenzy gradually subsided from its first turbulence, and at times she had even a dim recollection of the miseries which had befallen her. But these intervals were always brief, and she again, after a few minutes' apparent coherence relapsed into the dull sombre melancholy, which ever marks the victims of her distemper. Borgiano, though he strove when she was gay, to assume in her presence a gaity which his heart knew not, was in secret tormented with a thousand passions. Pity, and love, and sorrow at times melted his very heart within him; at others, a sort of un-directed rage swept away every softer feeling: till at length his whole soul settled in a burning and wreckless desire of vengeance, and Lanfranchi was its object. He had been present when Jacopo had uttered his last words. They had sunk deep into his heart at the time, and weighed heavily on his recollection now. Till at last he waited only for a fitting opportunity to hurl destruction on the head of a wretch whom the lips of a dying man had cursed.

As he walked one evening moody and melancholy along a quiet and retired quarter of the Lang' darno, he met with the object of his hate; swords were mutually drawn; and however Lanfranchi might have the advantage of his adversary in skill, Borgiano pressed upon him so furiously, that he rushed within his guard, and stabbed him to the heart. The weapon broke as the dying man staggered to the ground; and sheathing the remainder of his sword, the Florentine retired hastily from the spot. A crowd was speedily gathered to the scene. At first the name of Lanfranchi was on the lips of everyone; but when 'Florence' was decyphered in the faint light on the fragment of the weapon, which someone had extracted, still reeking and warm with blood, the sorrow of the people burst forth into tumultuous rage. 'Some accursed Florentine!' passed from man to man. – 'Down with the Florentine curs!' was next their cry; and when their minds were more settled, and they knew their own object, a search was commenced in the house of every Florentine family within the city. Borgiano, with that infatuation which seems ever to haunt men when engaged in the most desperate enterprises, had carried home with him the handle of the blade. It was stained with blood – the fragment corresponded with it exactly. These were damning proofs of guilt to the minds of the outrageous populace, to whom even more superficial evidence would have sufficed to convict any Florentine in their present ebullition of fury. They hurried him before judges who were not less prejudiced against him than his accusers; and as in those days proceedings against a criminal were brief in proportion as they were unjust; – his trial was concluded ere it was well begun. Death by the wheel was the sentence.

Maddalena, even in her lowliness and retirement, could distinguish the name of Borgiano uttered in curses fom Pisan tongues from every corner of the city. Roused by this into a state of excitement, restless, yet without an object, she escaped into the street; her dress in careless disarray, her hair untied, and her eye fixed in the wildness of unsettled thought. She wandered on through the people, an object of pity to some, of derision to others. She came, whether by instinct or chance, to the very spot where the whole circumstance of death was going on. Already had Borgiano's slow and terrible death been begun. He had endured the agonies of their most refined torture without gratifying their cruelty by uttering a single groan; and even the executioners, in spite of their hatred to his race, began almost to pity him, when they beheld one so young surrendering his life without a murmur.

Maddalena saw and recognized Borgiano as his limbs were writhing on the wheel. She rushed into the middle of the crowd – most of whom made way for her, as if unconsciously; others she tore aside, till she stood on the very spot where Borgiano was expiring on the rack; his eyes were then almost closed for ever – another turn of the wheel, and life was fled. Had Maddalena really recognized in him the companion of her moonlight wandering, the gentle wooer, whom even in her madness her soul had ceaselessly clung to? – For a while she stood motionless, as if gazing on the terrific sight before her, then fell to the ground stiff and moveless. Her heart had leapt for ever from its seat; and there she lay a cold and lifeless corpse, within a foot or two of Borgiano's mangled remains.

They were buried in the same grave by the kindness, or it may have been, by the derision of the Pisans. It was immediately under the hanging tower; and upon it some friend had placed a slab of polished marble, upon which the words 'Borgiano and Maddalena' were engraved. At the beginning of the last century it was still to be seen, though the ground had then gradually risen around it, and it was in some degree hid beneath a profusion of luxuriant wild flowers. Now it is completely lost to the sight, and no record remains to tell of their ill-fated love.

www.ingramcontent.com/pod-product-compliance
Lightning Source LLC
Chambersburg PA
CBHW030544180626
46810CB00005B/2002